Phonics Friends

Rusty on the Ranch
The Sound of **R**

The
**Child's
World**

By Cecilia Minden and Joanne Meier

The Child's World

Published in the United States of America
by The Child's World®
PO Box 326
Chanhassen, MN 55317-0326
800-599-READ
www.childsworld.com

The Child's World®: Mary Berendes, Publishing Director

Editorial Directions, Inc.: E. Russell Primm, Editorial
Director and Project Editor; Katie Marsico, Associate
Editor; Judith Shiffer, Associate Editor and School Media
Specialist; Linda S. Koutris, Photo Researcher and
Selector

The Design Lab: Kathleen Petelinsek, Design and Page
Production

Photographs ©: Corbis/David Stoecklein: 6; Corbis/D.
Robert and Lorri Franz: 14; Corbis/James L. Amos:16;
Corbis/John Lund: 18; Getty Images/Stone/Paul Harris:
8; Getty Images/Stone/Steve Bly: 12; Getty Images/
Taxi/James Randkley: 10; Photo Edit, Inc./Mary
Steinbacher: cover, 4; Romie and Alice Flanagan/
Flanagan Publishing Services: 20.

Library of Congress Cataloging-in-Publication Data
Minden, Cecilia.
  Rusty on the ranch : the sound of R / by Cecilia
Minden and Joanne Meier.
    p. cm. — (Phonics friends)
  Summary: Simple text featuring the sound of the letter
"r" describes Rusty's life on a ranch.
  ISBN 1-59296-304-8 (library bound : alk. paper)
[1. English language—Phonetics. 2. Reading.] I. Meier,
Joanne D. II. Title. III. Series.
PZ7.M6539Ru 2004
[E]—dc22   2004003538

Note to parents and educators:
*The Child's World® has created Phonics Friends with
the goal of exposing children to engaging stories and
pictures that assist in phonics development. The books
in the series will help children learn the relationships
between the letters of written language and the indi-
vidual sounds of spoken language. This contact helps
children learn to use these relationships to read and
write words.*

*The books in this series follow a similar format.
An introductory page, to be read by an adult, intro-
duces the child to the phonics feature, or sound, that
will be highlighted in the book. Read this page to the
child, stressing the phonic feature. Help the student
learn how to form the sound with her mouth. The
Phonics Friends story and engaging photographs follow
the introduction. At the end of the story, word lists
categorize the feature words into their phonic element.
Additional information on using these lists is on The
Child's World® Web site listed at the top of this page.*

*Each book in this series has been carefully written
to meet specific readability requirements. Close atten-
tion has been paid to elements such as word count,
sentence length, and vocabulary. Readability formulas
measure the ease with which the text can be read and
understood. Each Phonics Friends book has been ana-
lyzed using the Spache readability formula. For more
information on this formula, as well as the levels for
each of the books in this series please visit The Child's
World® Web site.*

*Reading research suggests that systematic phonics
instruction can greatly improve students' word recogni-
tion, spelling, and comprehension skills. The Phonics
Friends series assists in the teaching of phonics by
providing students with important opportunities to
apply their knowledge of phonics as they read words,
sentences, and text.*

This is the letter *r*.

In this book, you will read words that

have the *r* sound as in:

      ranch, ride, river, and *run*.

Rusty lives on a ranch.

This is his horse, Big Red.

Rascal

This is his dog, Rascal.

Rusty rides Big Red around the ranch. They like to ride along the river.

Rascal runs beside Rusty

and Big Red.

Rascal likes to chase rabbits.

The rabbits run away.

Rusty is learning to rope cattle.

It takes lots of practice!

It is starting to rain.

Rusty will return to the ranch.

Pretend you live on a ranch.

What would you like to do?

Fun Facts

If you hear someone talking about a kitten, you might assume that person is referring to a baby cat. But did you know that baby rabbits are also called kittens? Male and female rabbits are called bucks and does. The same names are used to describe male and female deer. Like cats, some rabbits make excellent family pets. But like deer, other rabbits are better off in the wild. You might think that rabbits are cuddly and adorable, but many farmers do not like wild rabbits because they eat crops.

You probably have heard of people riding horses. How would you feel about riding a camel or an elephant? People in Asia and Africa sometimes ride these animals, but horseback riding is more common in the United States. Athletes ride horses in races or as part of a sport called polo.

Activity

Horseback or Pony Riding

Have you ever ridden a pony or a horse? Sometimes town fairs feature pony rides, or maybe there is a stable in your area that offers horseback riding lessons. If you live near a local stable, ask your parents if you can visit and possibly speak with some of the people who work there. Before you ride a horse or pony, make sure you are comfortable around these animals and are familiar with important safety rules.

To Learn More

Books
About the Sound of R
Klingel, Cynthia, and Robert B. Noyed. *Rusty Red: The Sound of R.* Chanhassen, Minn.: The Child's World, 2000.

About Rabbits
Johnston, Tony, and Tomie dePaola (illustrator). *The Tale of Rabbit and Coyote.* New York: Putnam, 1994.
Rohmann, Eric. *My Friend Rabbit.* Brookfield, Conn.: Roaring Brook Press, 2002.

About Ranches
Noble, Trinka Hakes, and Tony Ross (illustrator). *Meanwhile Back at the Ranch.* New York: Dial, 1987.
Whitney, Gleaves, Louise Doak Whitney, and Susan Guy (illustrator). *B Is for Buckaroo: A Cowboy Alphabet.* Chelsea, Mich.: Sleeping Bear Press, 2003.

About Riding
Brett, Jan. *Armadillo Rodeo.* New York: Putnam, 1995.
McDonnell, Flora. *Giddy Up! Let's Ride!* Cambridge, Mass.: Candlewick Press, 2002.

Web Sites
Visit our home page for lots of links about the Sound of R:
http://www.childsworld.com/links.html

Note to Parents, Teachers, and Librarians: We routinely check our Web links to make sure they're safe, active sites—so encourage your readers to check them out!

R Feature Words

Proper Names

Rascal

Red

Rusty

Feature Words in Initial Position

rabbit

rain

ranch

return

ride

river

rope

run

About the Authors

Cecilia Minden, PhD, directs the Language and Literacy Program at the Harvard Graduate School of Education. She is a reading specialist with classroom and administrative experience in grades K–12. She earned her PhD in reading education from the University of Virginia. Cecilia and her husband Dave Cupp enjoy sharing their love of reading with their granddaughter Chelsea.

Joanne Meier, PhD, has worked as an elementary school teacher and university professor. She earned her BA in early childhood education from the University of South Carolina, and her MEd and PhD in education from the University of Virginia. She currently works as a literacy consultant for schools and private organizations. Joanne Meier lives with her husband Eric, and spends most of her time chasing her two daughters, Kella and Erin, and her two cats, Sam and Gilly, in Charlottesville, Virginia.